Once Upon An Iceberg

ERROL'S TWILLINGATE ADVENTURE

Sheilah Lukins

illustrated by Laurel Keating

" Errol is certainly no ordinary mouse, and his
surrender to the lure of adventure makes for an exciting,
effervescent tale that will charm readers of all ages. "

– ED KAVANAGH,
author of the *Amanda Greenleaf* series

" Young readers, eager to read chapter books,
will find the excitement of Errol's adventure,
the pacing of the story, and the varied
and interesting characterization fascinating. "

– JANICE FOSTER,
retired teacher and teacher-librarian
for *Canadian Review of Materials*

BREAKWATER
P.O. BOX 2188, ST. JOHN'S, NL, CANADA, A1C 6E6
WWW.BREAKWATERBOOKS.COM

COPYRIGHT © 2021 Sheilah Lukins • Illustrations © 2021 Laurel Keating
ISBN 978-1-55081-890-1

A CIP CATALOGUE RECORD FOR THIS BOOK IS AVAILABLE FROM LIBRARY
AND ARCHIVES CANADA

We acknowledge the support of the Canada Council for the Arts.
Nous remercions le Conseil des arts du Canada de son soutien.
We acknowledge the financial support of the Government of Canada and
the Government of Newfoundland and Labrador through the Department
of Tourism, Culture, Industry and Innovation for our publishing activities.
PRINTED AND BOUND IN CANADA.

Breakwater Books is committed to choosing papers and materials for
our books that help to protect our environment. To this end, this book is
printed on a recycled paper and other controlled sources that are certified
by the Forest Stewardship Council®.

To my grandchildren,

Jude and Dorian Harding,

and

Gavin, Ava and Ellivia Lukins.

May they read many books.

Chapter 1

A chilly night wind blew whitecaps across Conception Bay and the trees on Beachy Cove Drung swayed in the moonlight. Old Rat closed his suitcase and tied a scarf around his neck.

"When will you be back?" Errol pouted.

"In a few nights. I'm going to visit my cousins at Beachy Cove River."

Errol stomped his foot. "I want to go, too."

"Not this time." Old Rat picked up his suitcase.

A disappointed Errol waved goodbye to his friend as the first rays of sunlight peeped over the horizon. He wasn't ready for bed yet, even though the rest of his family were settling down for a good day's sleep. Wandering off into the long grass, he found a colony of ants. Just as he lay down to watch them, a thunderous bark made him jump. He heard heavy panting; the strong scent of dog was getting closer. He was trapped!

Errol backed into the shelter of a stone wall, closed his eyes, and waited for the dog to pounce. When he opened one eye to peek out, a large black nose and two big brown eyes stared down at him.

"Hi. How's it goin'? I'm Gus. I live down the lane with Brandon. What's your name?"

Slimy drool dangled from the dog's mouth, glistening in the sunlight.

"M-m-my n-n-name," Errol pressed closer to the wall, "is Errol."

"Would you like to play with me?" Gus grinned.

"Ah...I'd rather not." Errol's paws clutched at the rock.

Gus's head drooped. He looked so unhappy that Errol felt sorry for him. "How can we play when you're so big and I'm so small?"

"I could take you for rides on my back." Gus wagged his tail. "And I could take you to Twillingate with me. We're going to Granny Boyd's for the weekend."

"Twillingate?" Errol's insides bubbled with excitement. "I'd love to go to Twillingate. Hold on. I'll be right back." He darted across the driveway and squeezed underneath an old blue garbage box. The comforting smell of dark earth and rotting leaves greeted his nose.

Mother and Father had just put the last young mouse to bed. They looked over at Errol in surprise.

"What are you doing up this late?" Mother whispered.

Errol took a deep breath. "Mom. Dad. I've got a chance to take a trip. May I go? Please?"

"Oh, Errol. How far away this time?"

"Twillingate!" Errol's eyes shone.

His mother gasped. "I've never heard of it. It must be very far away."

Errol had no idea where Twillingate was, but the very name sent shivers of excitement down his spine.

Errol's father winked at him. "Now, Mother, Errol has proven he can handle himself in dangerous situations. Why, he went all the way to Gander last month and came home without a scratch."

"Very well." Errol's mother hugged him. "But be VERY careful. And don't forget—be kind and helpful whenever you can."

"I will..." he yelled, already heading out the door.

When Errol got back to the stone wall, Gus gave a happy bark. Errol climbed up a furry black leg to Gus's neck, where he nestled deep in the fur above the dog's bright orange collar. Together, they trotted down Beachy Cove Drung to Gus's house.

Chapter 2

"There you are." A blond-haired boy opened the back of a blue Jeep. "Jump in."

Errol's stomach lurched as the dog made a huge leap into the vehicle. When Gus settled, Errol poked his head up out of the dog's fur and looked out the back window. Brandon's dad was attaching a large open trailer to the Jeep. "What's that for?" Errol whispered in Gus's ear.

Gus shook his head. "Don't know. Never seen it before."

Errol scurried down Gus's leg to sniff around the Jeep for food. Munching on some cracker crumbs he found, he stared up at Gus. "What kind of a dog are you anyway?"

"I'm a mixed breed." Gus sat up very straight. "Mostly Newfoundland, but something else as well." His eyes saddened. "I never knew my father."

Errol thought of his own father, and sorrow for the big dog filled his heart. "Oh my. That's awful." He thought for a moment. "Where did your parents meet?"

"In Twillingate, on a visit to Granny Boyd's."

"Well," said Errol, tapping his chin, "maybe we can find your father when we get there."

Gus sighed. "They'll never let me off the leash."

"I'm not on a leash." Errol's face lit up. "I bet I could find your father. What does he look like?"

"My mother said he was very handsome. Black, with a white stripe like mine down his nose."

Errol stared hard at the large white patch on Gus's nose, and nodded.

For the rest of the trip, Errol dozed, and dreamed about how great it would be if he could locate Gus's father. He imagined the meeting between father and son, and how they would thank him and call him a wonderful mouse, smart and helpful. His mother would be so proud when he told her how hard he had worked to find Gus's dad.

When the family arrived in Twillingate, Brandon clipped Gus on to a long rope in Granny Boyd's garden and brought him a bowl of water and a dish of food.

Errol was hungry, too. He decided to go exploring.

"I'll be back in a bit."

"Slo-kay," Gus said, slobbering into his water bowl.

Errol headed down the main road. He found a discarded chip bag and ate the crumbs inside. Crossing the road, he scrambled down to a finger of beach near a big bridge.

Out in the water floated the most beautiful thing he had ever seen—a towering mountain of sparkling white ice. Old Rat had told him about icebergs.

"Icebergs are thousands of years old, Errol. They're white because the ice is filled with tiny air bubbles," Old Rat had explained. "They can be very dangerous. Just off our coast, a big ship called the *Titanic* hit one and sank."

Errol gazed at the berg, thinking how much fun it would be to slide down its icy slopes. All of a sudden, he heard a popping noise, followed by a long hiss. Next came a boom like thunder. Errol watched in horror as a chunk of iceberg slid into the sea, making it foam and bubble. Big waves rolled onto the shore. He jumped back in panic, but a wave caught him and pulled him out to sea.

"Help!" Errol cried. But no one answered, no one came to help.

"Put me back!" Errol screamed at the ocean. "PUT ME BACK!"

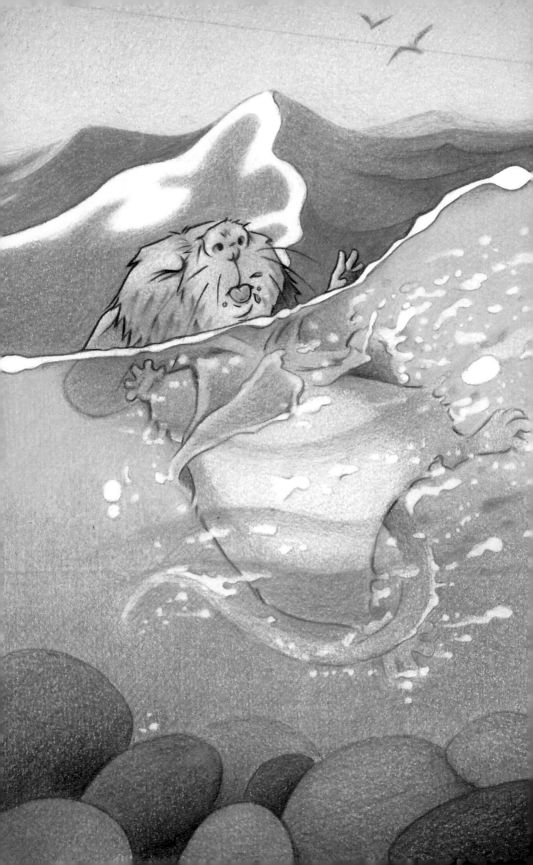

Chapter 3

The wave gathered power, and Errol sank into the salty water. He thought of his parents and how sad they would be when he didn't return.

Just when things looked hopeless, the wave lifted him up and charged back towards the rocky beach. The shore came closer and closer. Swoosh! Errol landed on a large clump of kelp.

He clung to the seaweed, but the water pulled hard at his feet.

"You're not getting me again!" he yelled.

"Come back, come back," the water seemed to say.

But Errol scrabbled over the kelp and started running. He didn't stop until he was safely out of reach of the sea.

On the rocky beach lay bottle caps, bits of rope, and even old sneakers. In amongst some pebbles, Errol spotted two glossy little blue shells. He slipped them in his jacket pocket, pleased with his find.

Climbing back up to the road to continue his search, Errol paused. His keen mouse ears picked up a snuffling noise. It was coming from behind a nearby house. Errol looked both ways, then dashed across the empty road. He didn't stop until he reached the back corner of the house. He peered around it—a large pit bull was working his way through a bowl of food. Errol gave a little cough. "Excuse me." He took a small step forward. "I'm looking for a dog with a white stripe down the front of his nose. Can you help me?"

The pit bull looked at him, an amused smile on his face. "Aren't you scared of me?"

"No," said Errol. "But I don't think I'll come any closer."

"Good idea." The pit bull returned to his dinner. A moment later, he looked up again. "Lots of dogs live on this road, but I don't know any with a white stripe. Try down by the wharf."

Errol thanked him and hurried off. Further down the road, he spied a man on the wharf splitting fish. Beside him sat a large black dog about the same size as Gus and with the same long curly hair.

Errol almost fell over in his rush to get closer. "Hello," he called out, breathless with excitement.

The dog turned to look at him.

Errol's heart sank. A pure black face stared back at him.

"Hello," she barked. "What are you doing out here? Aren't you worried a hawk will get you?" Errol looked up, but only seagulls wheeled far above.

"I'm looking for my friend's father," Errol said. "He's a black dog like you, but he has a white stripe on his nose."

The dog raised her eye whiskers. "I know a black dog with a white stripe. He lives in the grey house by the pizza shop. Keep going up this road."

When Errol got to the grey house, a furious barking erupted from inside. A door opened and a very small dog shot out.

"Gotta go. Gotta go," yipped the dog, running around in circles.

"Hey," yelled Errol. "Slow down!"

The little dog stood still, raised his leg, and stared at Errol. The dog had a long white stripe on his nose, but it was nothing like Gus's.

Finished, the little dog put his leg down and tore around in circles again, this time crying, "Gotta go in. Gotta go in." The back door opened and in he dashed.

Errol groaned. How was he going to find Gus's father?

Chapter 4

As he sat by the side of the house, Errol couldn't help but notice the wonderful smells coming from the pizza shop next door. His nose twitched and his stomach rumbled. One quick look inside for scraps wouldn't hurt. Eating might even make him think better. He darted around to the back entrance and slipped in unnoticed. Several silver bowls stood on a counter. Errol climbed up to take a closer look. One bowl smelled of mozzarella cheese. Delicious!

All at once a dark shadow fell across the counter.

Errol dived into a nearby pizza box. The lid closed and he felt the box move. He was being kidnapped by a pizza! Quivering in the dim light, Errol sobbed and sucked tomato sauce off his whiskers. His stomach always got him into trouble.

The box wobbled and shifted.

Errol heard a car door slam. He tumbled sideways as the car pulled out onto the road, with the pizza box and Errol inside. Finally they came to a stop. The doors creaked open. The box shifted again, and a warm blanket of pizza crust slid on top of Errol. Someone called out, "Come on, kids. Let's picnic up on the rocks by the lighthouse."

When the box came to rest, Errol slipped out from under the pizza, and lifted the lid a crack to peek out. The coast was clear. The people had gone to look at the icebergs. Errol dashed for cover into some nearby spruce trees and curled up in a snug hollow. Exhausted, he soon fell fast asleep.

An hour later, Errol stretched himself awake. "Where am I?" he wondered. Then he remembered his trip in the pizza box.

He crawled out of the hollow and climbed further up the rocky hill. He could see a parking lot full of people, cars, and dogs. But no Gus.

Behind Errol loomed a large white structure with a tall red-and-white tower. "That must be the lighthouse," he thought. Hungry again, Errol decided to look inside. He walked around the building— searching for a tiny crack in the wall, wide enough for a small mouse to slip through...there!

Errol squeezed inside. When his eyes adjusted to the darkness, he saw a shadowy shape. A voice hissed, "What are you doing in here?"

"Just looking for a quick bite to eat. Not staying." Errol's knees felt weak.

"Follow me," the old mouse muttered.

He led Errol into a grand hall under the floorboards. Mice lay in comfortable nests, napping and nibbling. Errol's stomach rumbled again.

A very large mouse lay in a nest, twice as big as the others.

Errol approached, hesitated, and then spoke in his loudest voice. "Hello, sir, sorry to wake you. My name is Errol, and I've come all the way from Beachy Cove, and..."

The big mouse looked at him in surprise.

"...I'm very hungry."

"Pull up an empty nest," boomed the head mouse. "My daughter Olivia will bring you something to eat."

A pretty young mouse ran into the shadows. She returned a minute later pulling a sandwich crust. When she smiled at Errol, his stomach did a flip-flop.

"What brings you here?" the head mouse asked him.

"I'm looking for my friend's father. My friend Gus is a dog, and his father lives somewhere in Twillingate. Or at least he used to. He has a white stripe down his nose, like this." Errol scratched a picture on the dusty floor. He stepped back and looked up at the head mouse. "Have you seen a dog with a stripe like that?"

The big mouse studied the picture, then shook his head. "Can't say I have."

Errol's shoulders slumped. "Thank you. You've been very kind, but I should get back to town. I have to find my friend Gus."

"Why not wait until your friend comes here? Everybody comes to Long Point Lighthouse. With so many icebergs around, he's sure to show up. And when you get back to town, visit the museum mice. They know *everyone*. They may be able to help you find Gus's father.

"I'll tell you what—tomorrow, we'll post sentries to watch for your friend."

"That would be great, sir." Errol's face broke into a grin. "Gus wears an orange collar. That should help the sentries spot him."

"That's sorted, then." The head mouse settled back in his nest. "In the meantime, Olivia will take care of you." He smiled at his daughter.

"Come on," said Olivia. "I'll show you something special."

Chapter 5

Olivia led Errol through passageways in walls and under floorboards, chattering as she went. "Did you know Twillingate, or Toulinguet, as the French called it, is two islands?"

Errol hurried after her. "What French?"

"French *people*, silly. Hundreds of years ago, they came here to fish. They called this place Toulinguet after islands in their country. When the English came, they couldn't pronounce the French word so they called it Twillingate.

"The famous opera singer Madame Toulinguet grew up in Twillingate." Olivia said, with a dreamy look in her eye. "I would love to be a famous opera mouse." She opened her mouth wide and let out several loud squeaks.

Errol cringed. "That would be...wonderful?" he murmured, following Olivia through a small hole into a huge open room.

"Shhh now," she held her paw up. "There might be tourists about."

The two mice raced down a long corridor and climbed a circular staircase. At the top stood a ladder. "Follow me," Olivia said. Errol was beginning to think she was a bit bossy.

They climbed up to the great light and ran to look out the curved glass walls. Ocean as far as the eye could see, and sitting in the middle of it, three glittering icebergs, golden in the evening sun.

"Aren't they beautiful," Errol sighed, reaching over to take Olivia's paw.

"What?" Olivia squinted. "I can't see a thing out there."

"Oh, right." He'd forgotten that Olivia, like most mice, couldn't see very well. Old Rat called Errol "an unusual case"—a mouse with excellent eyesight.

Heavy footsteps echoed through the lighthouse. Errol froze. They were coming up the stairs.

"Run!" Olivia squealed.

The two mice reached the ladder just as the lighthouse keeper's head came over the top step.

A big hand clamped down on them.

"Ha. I've got you."

Errol sank his teeth in the man's thumb. "Ouch," the keeper shouted, as he pulled his hand away. Down the ladder Errol and Olivia raced at lightning speed. They leapt on the railing of the circular staircase. Errol threw himself on his belly, copying Olivia, who was sliding at an alarming speed and yelling "Whee!" at the top of her lungs. Errol was too worried about falling off to enjoy the ride. Seconds later they landed in a heap at the bottom.

"Phew. That was close."

"Not at all," laughed Olivia.

They spent the rest of the night looking through garbage cans for food and touring the lighthouse. At dawn, they returned to the great hall.

After they had eaten, Errol and Olivia told everyone about the night's adventures. The head mouse called out in his loud voice, "Excellent, young Errol. Well done. Now to find your friend. We'll need sentries on the lookout for a large dog wearing an orange collar. Do I have any volunteers? You'll have to stay up all day. And no napping."

Quite a few young mice raised their paws. Under the supervision of older mice, they took up positions which gave them views of the parking lot. Operation Orange had begun....

Errol and Olivia hid in the grass beside the fence. The morning dragged on and on, with no sign of Gus.

"We have to get out of this heat," Olivia moaned.

"But Gus hasn't come yet. We can't leave." Errol felt a lump rise in his throat.

"We need water, and if we don't get better shade, we'll pass out. We could even die."

Errol tried not to show it in front of Olivia, but he was close to tears. What if he never saw Gus again? What if he never made it home to Beachy Cove?

Just then, a dog barked in the distance. Errol's ears perked up. The grass rustled nearby and a young mouse burst out squeaking, "Beachy Mouse. Beachy Mouse. Target spotted. Quadrant B. Go! Go! Go!"

Errol and Olivia ran like the wind.

"There's Gus." Errol skidded to a stop when he and Olivia reached the edge of the clearing.

Gus spotted them right away. "Hurry," he yipped, pulling on his leash. "We're going back to Granny Boyd's right now."

Errol turned to say goodbye to Olivia, but she pushed him forward. "I'm coming, too." Errol grinned, grabbed her paw, and they scrambled up Gus's leg.

When they got back to Granny Boyd's, Gus sighed as Brandon clipped him back on the garden rope.

"Don't worry, Gus," Errol said, as he and Olivia crawled out of the dog's fur and slid down his front leg. "Olivia and I will find your father."

"Don't be too long," Gus whined. "We leave for Beachy Cove tomorrow morning."

Chapter 6

Errol and Olivia were tired and hungry by the time they got to the museum. "Come on." Olivia tugged on his arm. "Let's visit my cousins. They'll have food, and they may know where to find Gus's father."

Slipping through a crack in the wall of the old building, they almost knocked over an elderly mouse.

"Auntie Rose!"

"Olivia," Great-aunt Rose squeaked in delight. "What are you doing so far from home? And who's this?"

"This is Errol, Auntie Rose. I'm helping him look for his friend's father." Olivia glanced over at Errol.

"We're looking for a dog with a white stripe down his nose." Olivia and Errol said together. "Father said you may know of a dog like that," Olivia added.

Great-aunt Rose paused for a moment. "Yes. There is a dog like that up behind the old house on the hill. But now is not a good time to go see him. Too many cats up that way this time of the evening. You can go in the morning."

Errol and Olivia looked at each other. Would they have time to find Gus's father and get back before the Jeep left?

"Don't even think about it." Great-aunt Rose put her paws on her hips. "Tomorrow. Now come eat and play with your cousins."

At dawn the next morning, Errol and Olivia headed up the road. Errol had a funny feeling in his stomach. This dog had to be Gus's father. The house, with its peeling paint and crooked windows, stood on a small hill away from everyone else. Errol and Olivia looked at it in dismay—did anyone even live there? All at once, they heard a bark, and then another. It reminded Errol of Gus's bark. "Come on," he called to Olivia. They streaked up the hill.

"It's coming from behind the house," Errol puffed. He and Olivia ran around the back.

A dog sat in an overgrown yard, tied to a stump. Although he was smaller than Gus, he was black and had a white stripe down the front of his nose identical to Gus's.

"It's him." Errol stared hard. "It has to be." His whiskers tingled with excitement.

Holding paws, he and Olivia inched towards the dog. When they were only a few feet away, the dog made a sudden lunge towards them. Olivia screamed.

"What are you doing on my land?" he growled, baring his teeth. The two mice flew down the driveway and didn't stop until they reached Granny Boyd's house.

Gus was pacing back and forth, talking to himself. Errol and Olivia ran up to him and collapsed at his feet. They were breathing so hard they couldn't speak for several minutes.

Gus looked at them, his eyes full of tears. "Thank goodness you're back. I overheard Brandon's parents talking. I know what the trailer is for. Granny Boyd's too old to live on her own. They're taking her and all her stuff back with us to Beachy Cove. This house is going to be sold, and we might never come back to Twillingate again. I'll never find my father!" Gus wailed.

"Gus, it's okay," Errol panted. "We think...
we think we've found him."

Gus gave a bark of joy and wriggled all over.
He tugged hard at the rope, and then flopped
on the ground.

"It's hopeless," he moaned.

Chapter 7

"No, it's not." Errol clicked his teeth together. "Come on, Olivia. Let's get chewing." The two mice started in on the rope. Soon only a few strands remained—Gus pulled and the rope fell apart.

"Jump on," he cried.

When they reached the old clapboard house, Gus came to an abrupt stop. "Do you think my family will go back to Beachy Cove without me?"

Errol could hear the panic in his voice. "They won't leave without you," Errol replied, with more confidence than he felt. "But we'd better be quick."

Gus hesitated. "You two wait here. I don't want to put you in any danger." With Errol and Olivia out of sight in the grass, Gus crept around the corner of the old house, head down and tail between his legs.

A moment later, Errol and Olivia heard fierce barking and then silence. Olivia began to cry.

"I'm going in." Errol's legs felt like jelly, but he knew he had to help Gus. Olivia wiped away her tears. "I'm coming, too," she said, in a thin, shaky voice. They edged towards the backyard.

Gus and the old dog stood a few feet apart, their ears flat back. The old dog's upper lip curled in a snarl and low growls came from deep in his throat. Gus looked miserable.

"Hold on, now," Errol called to the old dog. He was shaking so hard his teeth chattered. The dog looked down at Errol and Olivia.

"What do you want?" he roared, and gave a jump that brought the rope up short.

Errol almost fainted, but he managed to get the words out. "My friend here is looking for his father, and I'm helping him. We know his dad came from Twillingate, and since you are both black and have the same white stripe down your noses...well."

Errol let out a sigh of relief when he saw the old dog's ears go up. The dog stared hard at Gus's nose. He looked down at Errol, and said in a grumpy voice, "I don't know what my own nose looks like. How am I to know if they're the same markings?"

"Believe me..." said Errol.

"...they are." Olivia finished his sentence.

"Humph!" said the old dog. But he was looking at Gus with a small gleam in his eye.

"My mother is a Newfoundland dog, all black," Gus explained. "She used to come here in the summers and stay at Granny Boyd's house, in the cove."

Chapter 8

The old dog turned his head and gazed out at the ocean as if he were remembering something from a long time ago. His voice softened.

"Bella..."

Gus barked for joy. "Bella, yes—that's my mother's name."

The old dog stretched out his neck and nuzzled Gus's face. "I always wondered what happened to her. She left before we had a chance to say goodbye...I was sad for a long time afterwards."

Gus nodded. "My mother never forgot you either. She would sit on our back deck in Beachy Cove and tell me my father was a wonderful dog who lived far away in Twillingate."

The older dog gazed at him with eyes full of love and pride, murmuring, "Son...Gus." Just then the back door opened a crack and a feeble voice called out. "Jack. You okay?"

The dog gave two short yaps in reply and the back door closed.

Gus's tail wagged so hard it was almost invisible. "Errol here could chew through your rope," he panted. "You could come with us to Beachy Cove, you could..."

The old dog hesitated, then shook his head. "No thanks. I'll never forget you, son, but I can't leave my family. They are getting old, and need me to guard the property."

"Family!" Gus cried, remembering that his might leave without him. "We've got to go. Good-bye, Dad." The young dog gave his father a farewell nuzzle and a lick.

Errol climbed up on Gus, but Olivia remained in the grass.

"Aren't you coming?" Errol's heart sank.

"Not this time," Olivia said. "I'm going to stay with my cousins in the museum."

Errol got down again. He reached into his pocket and pulled out one of the lovely blue shells. "Here," he mumbled, the heat rising in his face. "For a beautiful mouse."

Now it was Olivia's turn to blush. "I'll always remember you, Errol." She kissed him lightly on the cheek.

Gus began to bark. "The Jeep. The Jeep. I saw it drive up the road. They must be looking for me. Let's go!"

Errol flew up to his spot above the orange collar and Gus took off down the road, his frayed rope trailing.

When they got to Granny Boyd's, there was no sign of the Jeep.

"They left without me." Gus threw his head back and howled.

"It's okay." Errol pointed to the full trailer. "They'll be..."

Before he could finish his sentence, the Jeep pulled into the garden and Brandon got out. "*Where* have you been? We've been looking all over for you." He gave Gus a fierce hug. While his father hitched the trailer on, Brandon helped Granny Boyd and Gus into the Jeep.

Hours later, tired but happy, Errol wriggled into his home under the old blue garbage box on Beachy Cove Drung. That morning around the supper table, Errol told the story of his adventure.

"And after the wave threw me back on shore, I found this." He placed the second blue shell on his mother's paw.

She gasped in delight, and stroked its satiny surface.

"Oh, Errol, it's beautiful...thank you. She gave him a warm hug and kissed the top of his head. "I am so proud of you, and so glad to have you home again."

About the Author

Sheilah (Roberts) Lukins is the author of three books for children: *Full Speed Ahead: Errol's Bell Island Adventure* (Winner of the 2018 Bruneau Family Children's/Young Adult Award), *Flying Ace: Errol's Gander Adventure*, and *Once Upon An Iceberg: Errol's Twillingate Adventure*. She has also written three non-fiction books for adults.

A lover of history, horses, dogs, good food, and great stories, Sheilah lives and writes in St. Philips, NL.

About the Illustrator

Laurel Keating is an award-winning artist whose work has adorned several Newfoundland children's books, including *Yaffle's Journey*, the *Find Scruncheon and Touton* books, *Moose's Roof*, *Elliot and the Impossible Fish*, *Nanny's Kitchen Party*, *Full Speed Ahead: Errol's Bell Island Adventure* and *Flying Ace: Errol's Gander Adventure*. *Once Upon An Iceberg: Errol's Twillingate Adventure* is her tenth book.

JOIN ERROL ON MORE ADVENTURES!

Be sure to read the other books in this series.

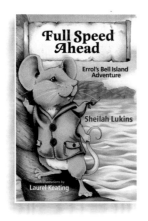

Full Speed Ahead:
Errol's Bell Island Adventure

WINNER of the 2018 Bruneau Family Children's/Young Adult Award

Flying Ace:
Errol's Gander Adventure

Canada Book Award WINNER

LONGLISTED for the 2020 Bruneau Family Children's/Young Adult Award